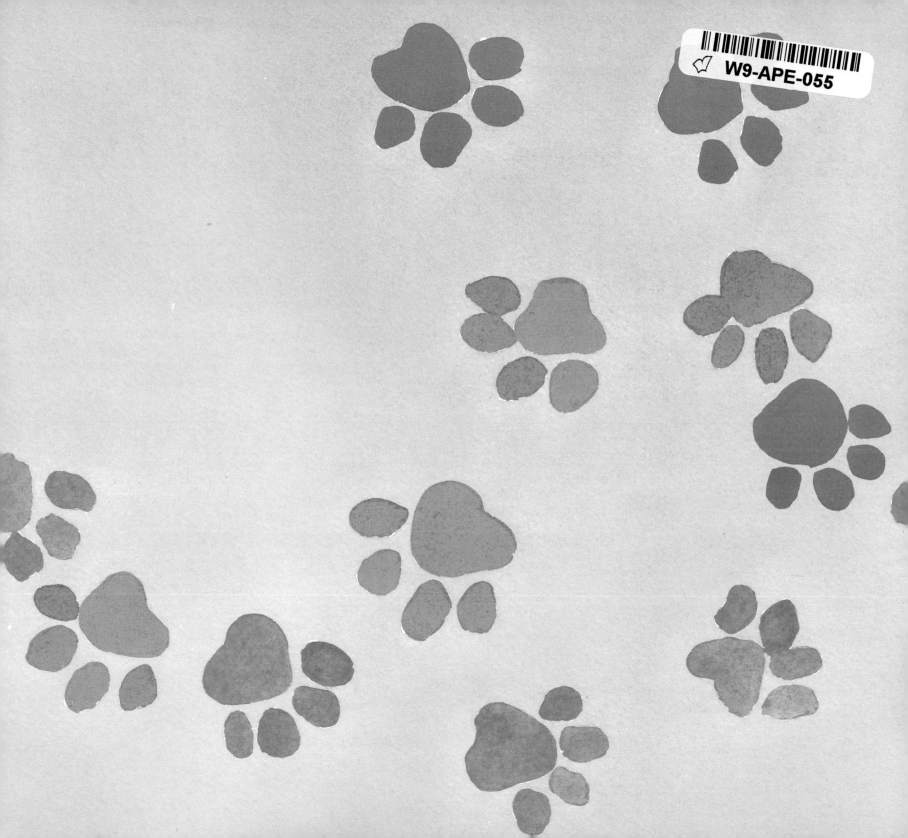

With love for my sister Ginny —C.W.M.

With love for Charles and Thomas —M.W.

With love for the 3 R's—
Running, Retrieving, and Recess —BOOMER

Book design by Suellen Ehnebuske/Lucy Nielsen.
Typeset in Syntax and Providance Sans.

No part of this publication may be reproduced in whole or in part, or stored in a retrieval system, or transmitted in any form or by any means, electronic, mechanical, photocopying, recording, or otherwise, without written permission of the publisher. For information regarding permission, write to Chronicle Books, 275 Fifth Street, San Francisco, CA 94103.

ISBN 0-590-99542-1

Text copyright © 1996 by Constance W. McGeorge.
Illustrations © 1996 by Mary Whyte.
All rights reserved. Published by Scholastic Inc., 555 Broadway, New York, NY 10012, by arrangement with Chronicle Books. TRUMPET and the TRUMPET logo are registered trademarks of Scholastic Inc.

12 11 10 9 8 7 6 5 4 3 2   7 8 9/9 0 1/0

Printed in the U.S.A.   08

First Scholastic printing, September 1996

Boomer Goes to School

By Constance W. McGeorge

Illustrated by Mary Whyte

Scholastic Inc.

New York   Toronto   London   Auckland   Sydney

Boomer was just settling down after his morning
walk, when suddenly, someone called his name.
Then, Boomer saw his leash.

Boomer was very excited—he thought he
was going for another walk.

But instead, Boomer and his owner raced outside, down the driveway, and onto a big yellow bus. Boomer was going for a ride!

The bus stopped again and again. Boomer had never been on a ride with so many children. The ride was very noisy.

After a while, the bus stopped in front of a big building.
The children climbed out. Boomer climbed out, too.
He was quickly led inside, up some stairs, around a
corner, and down a hallway.

Finally, Boomer's owner stopped at an open door.

Boomer looked in. It was a room filled with desks, tables, chairs, and children.

As Boomer was led to the back of the room, a loud bell rang. A grownup started talking. Everyone sat down and listened.

When the grownup finished talking, the children jumped up from their seats. Boomer was let off his leash. He didn't know what to do first!

There were toys to share . . .

. . . pictures to paint . . .

. . . games to play . . .

and best of all . . . there was lunch!

After lunch, Boomer watched as the children
gathered together and sat in a circle. Boomer
was ready for the next game. But this time,
all the children sat quietly.

Boomer started to get up, but he was told to sit down.

Boomer wiggled and squirmed. He was told to sit still.

Boomer barked and barked.
He was told to be quiet.

Boomer was very confused.

Then, Boomer was led to the center of the circle. He still wiggled and squirmed. Boomer's owner started talking—sharing stories about Boomer and showing him to the class.

Finally, Boomer understood. He sat still and stayed very quiet. Boomer's owner smiled and gave Boomer a big pat on the head!

Suddenly, a loud bell rang and it was time to take another bus ride. At each bus stop, Boomer's new friends patted him good-bye.

Then, the bus stopped at Boomer's house. Boomer wagged his tail and bounded off the bus for home.

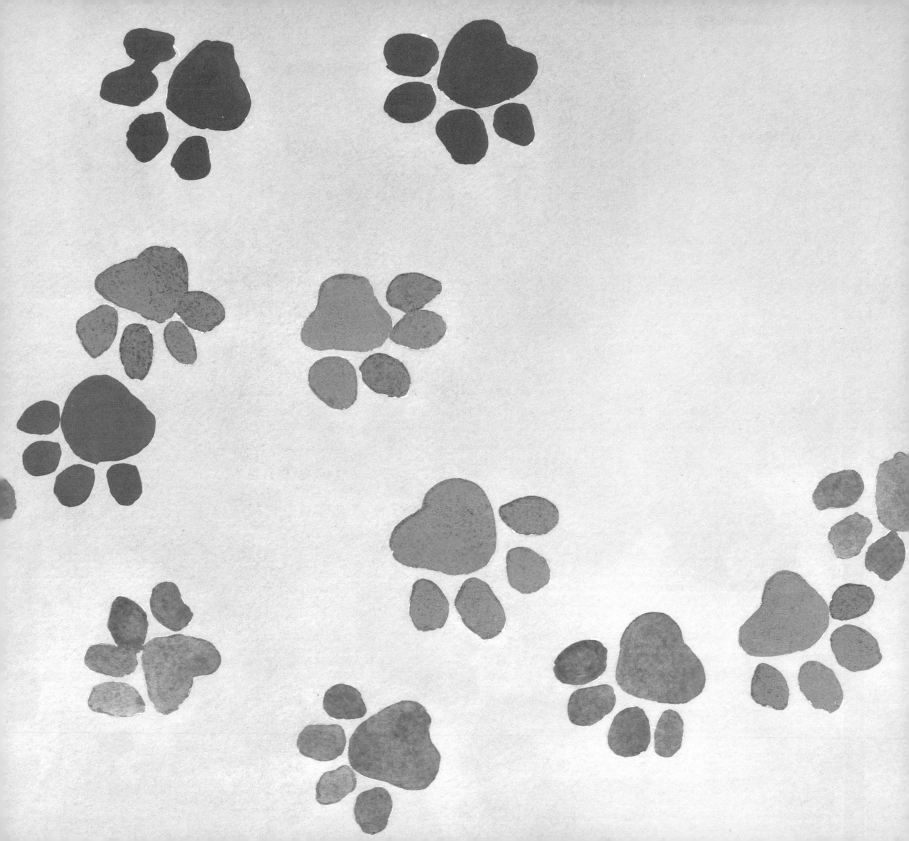

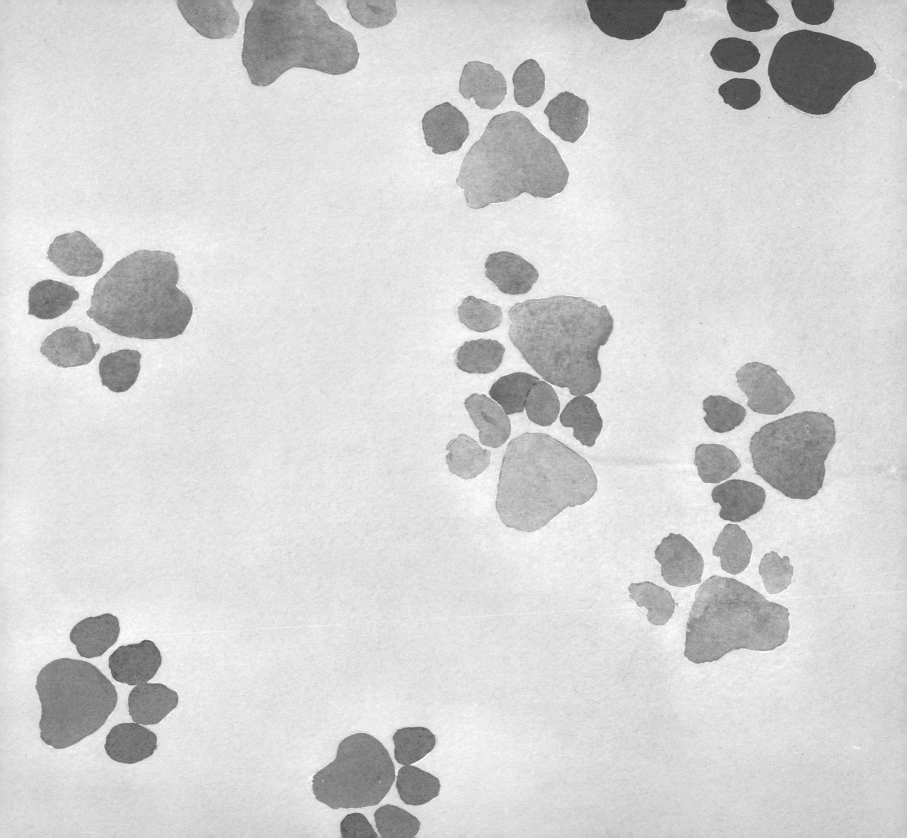